PUFFIN BOOKS

THE
MONSTER MUGGS

Jeremy Strong once worked in a bakery, putting the jam into 3,000 doughnuts every night. Now he puts the jam in stories instead, which he finds much more exciting. At the age of three he fell out of a first-floor bedroom window and landed on his head. His mother says that this damaged him for the rest of his life and refuses to take any responsibility. He loves writing stories because he says it is 'the only time you alone have complete control and can make anything happen'. His ambition is to make you laugh (or at least snuffle). Jeremy Strong lives in Kent with his wife, Susan, a cat or two, and something in the attic that makes scratching noises, but he hasn't found out what it is yet.

Some other books by Jeremy Strong

GIANT JIM AND THE HURRICANE
THE INDOOR PIRATES
THE INDOOR PIRATES ON TREASURE ISLAND
MY DAD'S GOT AN ALLIGATOR!
MY GRANNY'S GREAT ESCAPE
MY MUM'S GOING TO EXPLODE!
PANDEMONIUM AT SCHOOL
PIRATE PANDEMONIUM
THERE'S A PHARAOH IN OUR BATH!

Jeremy Strong

The Monster Muggs

Illustrated by
Nick Sharratt

PUFFIN BOOKS

Small monsters need big hugs – J.S.

PUFFIN BOOKS
Published by the Penguin Group
Penguin Books Ltd, 80 Strand, London WC2R 0RL, England
Penguin Putnam Inc., 375 Hudson Street, New York, New York 10014, USA
Penguin Books Australia Ltd, 250 Camberwell Road, Camberwell, Victoria 3124, Australia
Penguin Books Canada Ltd, 10 Alcorn Avenue, Toronto, Ontario, Canada M4V 3B2
Penguin Books India (P) Ltd, 11 Community Centre, Panchsheel Park,
New Delhi – 110 017, India
Penguin Books (NZ) Ltd, Cnr Rosedale and Airborne Roads, Albany,
Auckland, New Zealand
Penguin Books (South Africa) (Pty) Ltd, 24 Sturdee Avenue, Rosebank 2196, South Africa

Penguin Books Ltd, Registered Offices: 80 Strand, London WC2R 0RL, England

www.penguin.com

First published 2000
Published in this edition 2002
3 5 7 9 10 8 6 4 2

Text copyright © Jeremy Strong, 2000
Illustrations copyright © Nick Sharratt, 2000
All rights reserved

The moral right of the author and illustrator has been asserted

Printed in Hong Kong by Midas Printing Ltd

Except in the United States of America, this book is sold subject to the condition that it shall
not, by way of trade or otherwise, be lent, re-sold, hired out, or otherwise circulated without
the publisher's prior consent in any form of binding or cover other than that in which it is
published and without a similar condition including
this condition being imposed on the subsequent purchaser

British Library Cataloguing in Publication Data
A CIP catalogue record for this book is available from the British Library

ISBN 0–141–31575–X

The Monster Muggs were very
unhappy. They didn't like their cave.
It was cold and damp. The roof
leaked. Sometimes the wind howled
straight into their front room. The
cold made their feet turn blue. The
damp turned their noses red. The
wind gave them earache. It made
their teeth chatter.

"I don't like it in here," said Little Mugg. "All we have to keep us warm is one tiny candle. I'm cold." He pulled his big ears over his head like a blanket.

"I'm very cold," shivered Big Mugg. She wrapped her pigtails round her neck like a scarf.

"Well, I'm FROZEN STIFF LIKE AN ICICLE!" said Ugly Mugg, shaking his head crossly. "We can't stay in this cave any longer. We must find somewhere warm to live."

"Where can we go?" asked Little Mugg. "Nobody will let us live in a real house."

"We must find somewhere else then," said Ugly Mugg. "My bottom is so cold I think it's going to fall off!"

Ugly Mugg bent over the tiny candle, but his bottom did not feel any warmer. He bent lower. All at once his trousers caught fire.

"Oh! Ho! Eek!" he cried.

Ugly Mugg ran round the cave. Big Mugg and Little Mugg chased after him. They threw water at his trousers. There was a loud *sssss* and the flames went out.

"Oh dear," sighed Ugly Mugg. "Now I have a cold bottom, I've got a hole in my trousers and I'm soaking wet! It's no good. We must find a new house."

So the Monster Muggs set off to
find a new house.

"That old castle looks empty,"
said Ugly Mugg.

"That old castle looks creepy,"
said Little Mugg.

"It's a creepy-heapy!" said Big
Mugg. The Monster Muggs crept
inside.

Inside the creepy castle it was very
dark.

"Come on," said Ugly Mugg.
"We are brave monsters. This is a
good place to live. I'm not scared.
Are you scared, Little Mugg?"

"No," trembled Little Mugg,
covering his eyes with his great
big ears.

"Are you scared, Big Mugg?"

"No," shivered Big Mugg, covering
her eyes with her pigtails.

A spider dropped down from the ceiling. It landed on Little Mugg's head.

"Argh! A horrible spider!"

A bat came whizzing round the corner. It landed on Big Mugg's nose.

"Urgh! A horrible bat! I don't like it here!"

A mouse ran up Ugly Mugg's leg.

"Yeeek!" he squeaked. He turned very red and looked at the others.

"I'm not scared," he said. But he was!

AND THEN THREE SPOOKS
CAME INTO THE ROOM!!

"Whoo!" went Spooky One.

"Whoo-whooo!" went Spooky Two.

"Whoo-whooo-whoooooo!!" went
Spooky Three.

"Help!" cried Ugly Mugg. "I'm very scared now! Run for it!"

Little Mugg ran fast and Big Mugg ran faster, but Ugly Mugg was the fastest!

They didn't stop running until they came to a farm. They sat down inside a barn.

"This is better," said Ugly Mugg. "It's nice and quiet in here."

"Honk, honk!"

"Argh! It's a flappy monster with pecky bits," said Big Mugg, and she ran away.

"Moo!"

"Argh! It's a spotty monster with wobbly bits," cried Little Mugg, and he ran away.

Ugly Mugg ran after them. He didn't like being in there on his own.

Ugly Mugg had a bright idea.
"I know somewhere that's warm and
dry. There is plenty of food too.
Let's go to the school!"

"Jelly brain!" cried Big Mugg.
"We can't go there. The school is full
of children."

"No problem! We shall scare them all away," said Ugly Mugg. "We shall pull nasty faces and make horrible noises. The children will be so frightened, they will run away. We shall have the whole school to ourselves. It will be easy."

"Easy-peasy!" laughed Little Mugg.

"Easy-peasy, no more freezy!" shouted Big Mugg.

They set off down the hill.

Down at the school, the playground was full of children. They were running around and laughing and playing. The Monster Muggs hid behind a bush.

"When I say 'GO' we must jump out and frighten them," said Ugly Mugg.

"OK," said Little Mugg.

"Okey-dokey, what a jokey!" said Big Mugg, laughing.

Ugly Mugg got ready. "GO!" he yelled.

The Monster Muggs jumped up
from behind the hedge. They ran to
the playground and they pulled
horrible faces.

"BOO!" cried Little Mugg.

"BIG BOO!" bellowed Big Mugg.

"BIG BAD BOO!" shouted
Ugly Mugg, and he made himself go
cross-eyed. He stuck out his tongue.
He pulled out his ears until they hurt.

The children stopped running around the playground and they stared at the Monster Muggs.

"What are you doing?" asked Lucy.

"We're making nasty faces!" growled Ugly Mugg.

"Why are you making nasty faces?" asked Ravi.

"Because we are so scary you are going to run away!" yelled Ugly Mugg.

"You're not scary," said Tracey.

"We're not?" The Monster Muggs were very surprised.

"No, you're not," shouted the children.

"This is scary," said Ben, and he pulled a truly horrible face.

"Aaargh!" cried Big Mugg, jumping back.

"This is scary too," said Anna, and she stuck out her tongue.

"I want my mummy!" yelled Little Mugg. He jumped back, right into Big Mugg's arms.

"And this is even scarier," said Tom. He put his fingers in his mouth and pulled his lips wide.

"Let's get out of here!" screamed
Ugly Mugg. He jumped right back
into Little Mugg's arms.

Big Mugg ran and ran. She was
still carrying the other two Muggs,
and the children chased after them.
Big Mugg ran round to the back of
the school.

"Quick, hide in here!" cried Ugly Mugg. They jumped inside a giant rubbish bin and hid beneath the rubbish.

"Phew!" sighed Big Mugg. "We're safe now."

Ugly Mugg looked round the inside of the bin. It was dark and warm inside. There was no wind freezing his bottom off. There was no rain dripping through the roof. He looked at Big Mugg and Little Mugg and gave them a big smile.

"Welcome to our new home!" he said.